OPEN WORLD SQUAD

▶▶ LEVEL UP ◀◀

BY MICHAEL ANTHONY STEELE

ILLUSTRATED BY MIKE LAUGHEAD

raintree 🍃

a Capstone company — publishers for children

Raintree is an imprint of Capstone Global Library Limited, a company incorporated in
England and Wales having its registered office at 264 Banbury Road, Oxford, OX2 7DY –
Registered company number: 6695582

Designed by Heidi Thompson
Original illustrations © Capstone Global Library Limited 2025
Originated by Capstone Global Library Ltd

978 1 3982 5749 8

British Library Cataloguing in Publication Data
A full catalogue record for this book is available from the British Library.

Printed and bound in India.

CONTENTS

OPEN WORLD

In this online video game, players are free. Be whatever avatar you want. Team up with whoever you want. Choose any type of mission you want! Fantasy adventure, battle racing, sci-fi, action and more. So log on . . .

Open World awaits!

THE SQUAD

Kai

Screen name: K-EYE
Avatar: Techno-Ninja
Strengths: Supply,
Stealth

Kai doesn't like being the centre of
attention. He chose a role in OW where
he can help others – in the background.
His ninja avatar has many pockets to hold
the squad's gear. Kai takes the job very
seriously. He is quick to rush into a fight
and pass out anything the group needs.

Hanna

Screen name:
hanna_banana
Avatar: Elvin Archer
Strengths: Speed,
Long-Range Attacks

Hanna is often busy with her school's drama
department. She first joined OW to spend
more time with her best friend, Zoe. In OW,
she's great with a bow and arrow. Hanna
is thrilled to take on a big role during the
squad's attacks.

Mason

Screen name: MACE1
Avatar: Robo-Warrior
Strengths: Leadership,
Close-Range
Attacks

Mason knows the value of teamwork.
So he and his best friend, Kai, teamed up
in OW with cross-country friends Hanna
and Zoe. Mason has a strong avatar. But his
true strength? Acting as squad leader and
bringing together the players' many skills.

Zoe

Screen name: ZKatt
Avatar: Feline Wizard
Strengths: Spells,
Defence

Zoe is a tech wizard and OW expert.
She has been playing the longest out
of the squad. Her avatar's magic and
defence skills help to keep the group
safe. Zoe isn't quite a pro gamer. But
she's close! Hundreds of followers
watch her live streams.

CHAPTER 1

MASSIVE MISSION

Zoe leaned in. The opening cut scene filled her computer screen. The video clip showed a giant robot. It was falling from the sky.

BOOOOM!

The scene shook as the robot landed in a crouch. It slowly stood. The thing was as big as Godzilla! The robot took a lumbering step forwards. Its target? A futuristic city on the horizon.

Zoe lowered the mic on her headset. She looked into her webcam.

"Are you ready, Z-peeps?" she asked her followers. "If you're new to Open World, here's the lowdown on this level. The evil robot Rommix plans to destroy the city of Lexira. Who's gonna stop it? Just the best OW squad ever! My squad!"

Zoe had been live streaming video games for almost a year now. The thirteen-year-old had built up a pretty good following. She smiled as she checked the view counter. Hundreds of fans were watching at that very moment!

Open World was Zoe's favourite thing to play. The online video game had loads of missions. Players could search castles in fantasy levels. Race in wild battle courses. Or take on giant robots in sci-fi levels like this one.

Zoe's followers liked the mix too. She read their comments in a chat window on her second computer screen. They were cheering on her and her teammates.

"Thanks, FlyAway. Thanks, Ducky," she replied. "We won't let you down!"

Zoe didn't have time to read all the comments. She mainly focused on the gameplay. And when she streamed with her squad? There was a second chat window to read. A private one. The one her squad used.

> **K-EYE:** So just the four of us vs one huge robot. NBD huh?

> **MACE1:** nothin we cant handle!

> **hanna_banana:** >:)

Zoe typed a reply.

> **ZKatt:** we r live so lets make it good!

Four avatars showed up on the screen. Zoe and her squad were in a town not far from Rommix. They zipped towards the huge robot on hover scooters.

Zoe got a feel for the controls. Her cat-like avatar swayed from side to side. Ahead of her, the tall Elvin avatar pulled out a rocket launcher. The Elf aimed at Rommix.

FWOOSH! A rocket shot into the air. It left a long, winding trail of smoke.

BOOM! It blew up on the robot's side.

But the giant kept moving. No damage!

> **ZKatt:** didnt think it was going 2 b that easy did u?

> **hanna_banana:** lol guess not but had 2 try :)

That was Zoe's best friend, Hanna. Her Elvin avatar was best for long-range attacks. She could easily hit a target with a bow and arrow. Or a rocket launcher!

Rommix slowly spun its head around. **ZZZZZT!** Lasers blasted from its eyes. The red-hot beams shot towards the squad.

Mason's robot-head warrior was at the front. He dodged just in time. The road exploded right beside him. Chunks of concrete went flying.

Zoe speeded over and turned on her shield. **WOMP!** A shining blue circle of energy kept Mason safe from the rubble.

The robot turned back towards the city.

MACE1: that was close! thx Z

hanna_banana: sorry 4 making the bot mad M!!!

MACE1: yeah... mybe save the rockets til we r closr

Mason often led their missions. He was great at coming up with plans of attack. He knew how to use everyone's strengths.

Zoe and Hanna had met Mason and his friend Kai online a few months ago. They had teamed up for an OW mission. Then that was it. They knew they had the perfect squad!

MACE1: hey K look around. there has 2 b somethng we can use 2 fight ths thing

K-EYE: Will do!

Kai's techno-ninja avatar split off from the others. Kai was in charge of the squad's supplies. Important items were often left around OW levels. Kai was great at finding them.

The rest of the squad zipped towards the robot. Zoe frowned as they got closer.

ZKatt: that bot is SO BIG... maybe this wasnt the best levl to stream

MACE1: no worries, we will figure it out Z

hanna_banana: totes! we always do

K-EYE: Found something!

hanna_banana: ??

Kai raced towards a broken shop window. Something was glowing inside. He used a grappler to grab it.

MACE1: so???

K-EYE: Magnetic boots! Four pairs!

hanna_banana: YESSSS! u know what this means

Zoe sighed with relief. She did know.

"These mag boots must be key in fighting Rommix," she told her followers. "Looks like we're going for a climb. Up the robot! Yeah!"

CHAPTER 2

GOING UP!

Kai handed out the magnetic boots to the squad. Then they raced closer to the lumbering robot.

The ground shook with Rommix's every step. The shaking didn't affect the players' hover scooters. But they had to dodge all the rubble being kicked up by the giant feet. Zoe blocked the larger pieces with her shield.

K-EYE: We got the mag boots. But how do we climb onto the bot without getting stomped?

hanna_banana: flying spell Z? To get over its feet?

ZKatt: wont work here

Zoe's cat avatar was a wizard. In fantasy OW levels, she could use lots of spells. Some for attacks. Others for defence. But most were useless in sci-fi levels.

Mason speeded ahead. He turned towards a tall bridge in the robot's path.

> **MACE1:** go 4 the overpass! we cn use it 2 jump on the bot!
>
> **hanna_banana:** good 1!!!
>
> **K-EYE:** Isn't he going to step on it?
>
> **MACE1:** have 2 time it jst right

The squad followed Mason's lead. They passed Rommix and went onto the motorway.

ZZZT! ZZZT!

Rommix shot at them with its laser eyes. The squad dodged the blasts. They kept going. They followed the road up the overpass.

The robot stomped closer. It was on a direct path for the road!

MACE1: faster!

ZKatt: get ready 2 jump!

hanna_banana: WEEEEEE

They poured on the speed. Rommix was right over them now.

CRASH! Its huge foot smashed into the overpass.

Mason was the first one there. He raced off the broken structure. Pushed off the scooter. Sailed towards the robot's ankle.

SHWOOMP! His magnetic boots stuck to the metal surface.

Rommix raised its other foot. Chunks of rubble rained from above. Zoe powered on her shield. She kept the others safe as they raced forwards.

Hanna and Kai jumped. **SHWOOMP!**
SHWOOMP! They made it onto the robot!

Zoe lowered her shield. She jumped just as the last of the overpass fell away. **SHWOOMP!**

The view on Zoe's screen shifted. Everything spun as she stood on the robot's outer shell.

K-EYE: Oh boy. Motion sickness.

ZKatt: just keep looking at the robot and not the topsy-turvy world

K-EYE: Don't say topsy-turvy LOL.

ZKatt: lol sorry!

hanna_banana: so now what???

MACE1: the bot is 2 big 2 jst start attacking

ZKatt: maybe we gotta get inside and find a weak spot? take it down from there?

hanna_banana: ooo ya! like a nasty robot virus!!!

K-EYE: I bet we have to go to the head. It's always the head.

MACE1: good idea, lets get going

Mason led them up the robot. The new setting was strange. Huge gears, resistors and transformers covered the metal surface.

"Pretty wild, huh?" Zoe asked her followers. "We're walking up a robot like a flea!"

K-EYE: We must be going the right way. There's a save point.

hanna_banana: uh oh

Some OW missions had clear save points. They were glowing red circles on the ground. If the squad got game over, they restarted from there. A save point often meant danger was just ahead.

Hanna had been right to worry. The squad moved over the save point. As soon as they did, a laser turret rose from a hidden hatch.

ZZZT-ZZZT! ZZZT-ZZZT! ZZZT-ZZZT!

The squad hid behind a transformer.

hanna_banana: plan?!

MACE1: hey actually can we call it?

ZKatt: gotta get dinner for little bro?

MACE1: u know it

hanna_banana: microwave king!!!

MACE1: lol thats me

K-EYE: Tell Devon hi!

ZKatt: same time tomrrw?

hanna_banana: OH YEAH! im gonna get homework done early for a full night of gaming

MACE1: yeah we gonna figur out how 2 beat the bot!

K-EYE: Bye!

hanna_banana: ttfn!!!

ZKatt: cu!

Zoe left the level. The Open World logo filled her screen. She looked into the webcam.

"Sorry, peeps," she said. "We'll pick this one up again tomorrow. But how cool was that? OW has cranked things up to eleven!"

She read her followers' chat.

FlyAway: <3

DRRY: AW!!! wanna c what happens next!

wurmee: i wud use mor rockets

lemonHD: has 2b a way inside tht thng

BossFght: take out its batteries lol

Ducky: is someone driving it?

1VICTORY1: be cool if you could drive it!!

RedRhino44: 2 scared 2 keep going? u guys r noobs

Zoe's lips tightened. "Hey, RedRhino44," she said. "Don't dis my squad. Or I will *so* block you. People have lives, you know."

Zoe was about to read more chats. Then another window popped up. It was a direct message. Her breath caught in her throat.

The DM was from TerryT3. He was part of a pro gamer team called Triple-T. Zoe watched their streams all the time.

TerryT3: GG ZKatt! Big fan of yur stream AND yur skillz. Want to guest on TTT? We are about to move up that robot!

Zoe couldn't believe it. She was being asked to play with a pro gamer team. And not just any team. One of her favourites!

Zoe didn't give it a second thought. "Guess what, Z-peeps?" she said. "I'm going to keep fighting Rommix after all!"

CHAPTER 3

BOSS LEVEL

"You should've seen it, Dad," Zoe said between bites. She barely swallowed before continuing. "Me playing with Triple-T. It was amazing!"

Zoe's dad sat across from her at the dinner table later that evening. He raised an eyebrow. "And who are these Triple-T people again?" he asked.

"A pro gamer squad," Zoe said. "They're total GOATs in Open World!"

Her dad shook his head. "Wait. They're goats?"

"Goat Simulator?" her little brother, Zach, asked. "I've heard of that game."

Zoe laughed. "Not that kind of goat. It stands for greatest of all time."

"Oh, of course," Dad said. Then he turned to Zach. "There's a goat simulator game?"

Zach nodded.

"There's a game for almost anything, Dad," Zoe said. "But anyway, Triple-T are mega-stars. I got loads more followers just playing with them once."

"As long as you had fun," Dad said.

Zoe looked at her plate. "If I get more followers, I could even go pro."

Her dad put his fork down. "Now, we've talked about this," he said. "I think you spend too much time on the computer as it is."

"Going pro sounds cool!" Zach said. "I wish I could play video games all day."

"It's not just about playing," Zoe explained. "You have to be part of gamer groups. Which I am. You have to stream. Which I do." She sighed. "I just need to put in more time. Get even more followers. Then I could get sponsors and –"

"Zoe, maybe when you're older, we can talk more about this," Dad said.

"But there are a bunch of pro gamers my age," Zoe argued. "Some even quit school to play full time."

"Quit school?" Zach asked with wide eyes. "I'm in!"

"Absolutely not," Dad said.

"Some are home-schooled," Zoe added.

"And who's going to do that?" Dad asked. "I'm busy pulling extra shifts at work as it is."

Zoe shrugged. "I . . . I could help with that. I know things are tight. But pro gamers get sponsors. They get paid real money."

"No school *and* you get paid to play?" Zach asked. "We could both –"

"Not now, Zach," Zoe and her father said together.

Dad sighed. "Look, Zoe. Right now, you need a normal life with normal friendships. If you want to shut yourself away on the computer all day once you're grown, I can't stop you."

Zoe shook her head. "Is that really what you think I do? I have normal friendships! And thanks to gaming, I have friends all over the country!"

"It's not the same," Dad said.

Zoe opened her mouth to argue. But she stopped herself. Her dad just didn't get it. She stirred the rest of her dinner with her fork. She suddenly wasn't hungry.

CHAPTER 4

BIG NEWS

The next night, Zoe met her squad in OWM, the Open World Market. Here, players could buy all kinds of items and upgrades. The squad was still in the middle of a level. So they couldn't pick up more supplies. But OWM was a great place to chat before the action. Zoe had a lot to tell her friends.

hanna_banana: your dad ttly doesnt get it

MACE1: how r we not real friends??

K-EYE: I talk to you three more than anyone IRL.

hanna_banana: and u all got me thru auditions with my last play!!!

MACE1: plus who am i gonna rant 2 when Devon is being a pain lol

hanna_banana: lol!

ZKatt: u guys r srsly the best! but it was my fault w/ my dad. brought up going pro again

hanna_banana: ouch

MACE1: duznt he know u stream already?

ZKatt: yeah but he doesnt rly get how it all works

hanna_banana: u still gonna stream this next 1?

ZKatt: if thats ok?

K-EYE: Sure!

hanna_banana: yup!!!

MACE1: then lets do this!

As the squad left OWM, Zoe realized something. She hadn't told her friends the bigger news. Playing with Triple-T! She had been too busy venting about her dad. She would have to tell them at the next save point.

Zoe began the stream. "Hey, Z-peeps," she said. "If you were here last night, we're gonna have a repeat. But now it's ZKatt and her squad versus Rommix the robot. Who's with me?"

The followers' chat began filling up.

lemonHD: ttly!

wurmee: use mor rockets tho

DefRon1: go 4 it!!

Zoe started the level. A familiar scene filled her screen. The squad stood on the robot's leg. They each wore mag boots. They stood in the save circle.

MACE1: rdy for that lazer?

hanna_banana: I got this!!!

Hanna took out a rocket launcher. She stepped forwards, and the laser turret popped up. Hanna fired. The turret exploded before it had even fired a shot.

ZKatt: gg H!

K-EYE: Yeah!

hanna_banana: >:)

MACE1: lets keep mvn!

The squad sneaked around giant metal gears. They came across three more turrets. Hanna took out two. Mason blew one up with his laser rifle.

The squad reached the robot's torso. As soon as they did, four hatches opened. Drones flew out.

ZZZT-ZZZT! ZZZT-ZZZT!

Laser beams rained down on the squad.

Hit! Hit! Hanna and Mason took damage. But then Zoe powered on her shield. The rest of the lasers bounced off the blue circle of light.

ZKatt: this wont hold 4 long

MACE1: K medpack!

Kai rushed in. He gave med packs to Mason and Hanna. Their health bars shot up to full.

Mason ducked out from the shield. He tried to blast a drone. Miss! Hanna fired a rocket. Miss!

hanna_banana: they r 2 fast!

ZKatt: H blast that green hatch to yur right

hanna_banana: rly??

ZKatt: yeah hurry!

Hanna blew the hatch open. A tunnel was behind it. Leading right into the robot.

ZKatt: n2 there!

They ran for the tunnel. The drones kept firing. But Zoe kept her shield up. She kept the squad safe. One by one, they dropped inside. Zoe went in last. Her shield fizzled out just as she did.

The squad stood in a long hallway. They stepped into a save point.

hanna_banana: good idea Z!!!

ZKatt: yeah! its a shortcut to the bots back

K-EYE: Nice!

MACE1: how did u know bout it?

Zoe smiled. With the break in action, she could finally tell her friends the big news. Her fingers raced over the keys.

ZKatt: with all the dad drama i forgot 2 tell u, i teamed up w/ TTT last night!!!

K-EYE: Triple-T?? Wow!

hanna_banana: wait

hanna_banana: u played ahead without us?

ZKatt: just a little, didnt finish the level. TTT showed me this shrtcut

MACE1: thot WE were yur squad

ZKatt: u r!! but they invited me 2 guest on their team

K-EYE: Great break if you ever go pro!

ZKatt: thats what i thought! how could i say no???

MACE1: thnk im dun playin tonite

hanna_banana: me 2

ZKatt: rly?

MACE1: yeah l8r

K-EYE: Ok, bye I guess.

Hanna's avatar faded away first. The others soon followed.

Zoe left the level too. She stared at the OW logo. The image blurred as tears filled her eyes.

"Sorry, Z-peeps," she said. "That's all for now. See you tomorrow."

She stopped the stream. She didn't have the heart to check her followers' chat.

CHAPTER 5

SCHOOL CHAT

The next morning, Zoe felt sick to her stomach.
But she still went to school. It wasn't that kind of sick.
She felt crummy because her friends were angry
with her. And to be honest, she was a little angry too.

Her friends knew her dream was going pro.
They all knew how big Triple-T was in gaming.
Mason and Hanna should have been happy for her.
Why couldn't they be like Kai? He got it.

If Hanna still went to Zoe's school, she could
talk to her best friend. Face-to-face. But Hanna had
moved away to live with her grandparents.

So now the girls usually chatted in the OW mobile app. They still had the same lunch time. They caught up then. Zoe wondered if Hanna would even chat with her today.

The morning dragged by. Finally, lunchtime came. Zoe logged in. To her surprise, Hanna was online too.

ZKatt: hey

hanna_banana: hey

ZKatt: look im sry about playing ahead

hanna_banana: u should b. what were u thinking?

ZKatt: about going pro. u know thats the dream

hanna_banana: so u r just gonna ditch yur friends???

ZKatt: come on H

hanna_banana: u r the one who sneaked off and didnt tell us about it

ZKatt: i DID tell u tho, wasnt a secret

ZKatt: tbh thought u wud be more supportive

hanna_banana: i do support u, just shocked by the betrayal

ZKatt: betrayal?!

hanna_banana: low-key but still

hanna_banana: since i moved this is all we have u know? and u ditched it for what? mor views?

ZKatt: i wudnt ever ditch u guys! but u of all pple know how hard my dad has 2 wrk now. goin pro wud let me help. by doin something im good at

hanna_banana: i get it. i do.

hanna_banana: still stings tho

ZKatt: how bout this

ZKatt: i promise never to play ahead in the same level w/o u? even if TTT asks again

hanna_banana: that would b nice

ZKatt: deal!

hanna_banana: gotta get 2 class

ZKatt: we good?

hanna_banana: yeah

hanna_banana: sorry i got so mad

hanna_banana: <3

Zoe let out a sigh of relief as she logged off. She slipped her phone into her backpack. Her lunch period was almost over too.

As she walked to class, Zoe was glad that Hanna wasn't angry any more. Hopefully, Mason would come around too. But part of Zoe wondered. Could she really say no if Triple-T asked again? It *had* been a huge bump with her levelling up to pro.

Zoe shook her head. The invite was probably a one-time thing. She doubted she would have to make that choice again.

CHAPTER 6

NO SHORTCUTS

That night, Zoe logged on to OW. She didn't start the stream. She wanted to chat with her squad first.

Her avatar stood in the metal hallway inside the robot. The others soon popped up around her.

ZKatt: M im sorry i went ahead. i didnt thnk about u guys feeling left out

MACE1: its ok. K and me were talkin. reminded me how important going pro is 2 u

hanna_banana: i needed reminding 2!!!

K-EYE: So... how was playing with TTT?

ZKatt: pretty sweet! but not as fun as w/ u guys!

hanna_banana: :)

ZKatt: wuz thnkng. what if we go back out

K-EYE: Back to those drones?

hanna_banana: what about the shortcut?

ZKatt: forget it. lets go up anothr way so we can do it 4 the first time together

hanna_banana: <3

K-EYE: Nice.

MACE1: im game, lets gooo!

Zoe began streaming. "All right, Z-peeps," she said. "My squad's ready to go. But we're leaving the shortcut I took with Triple-T. We still think reaching the robot's head is the goal. But we're finding our own way. Time to lace up those mag boots again!"

Zoe was about to check her followers' chat. Then a movement caught her eye.

Her dad was standing in her bedroom doorway. Zoe gave a quick wave. Dad sighed. Waved back. Then shook his head and walked away.

Zoe wondered what he was thinking. With all that talk about a robot's head. She couldn't worry about that now. She got into the game with her squad.

Zoe went through the hatch first. As soon as she was outside, she brought up her shield. **WOMP!**

The drones attacked. **ZZZT-ZZZT!**

But Zoe's shield blocked the lasers. The others safely climbed out. Mason shot his laser rifle. Hanna fired her rocket launcher.

BOOM! BOOM-BOOM-BOOM!

The drones were toast.

K-EYE: Well that wasn't as bad as I remember it.

MACE1: cuz r squads the best

hanna_banana: WOOT WOOT

ZKatt: then lets beat this thng!

The squad moved up Rommix.

WHOOOOOOSH!

A huge metal object suddenly rushed towards them. The thing wasn't a drone. It was the robot's clawed hand. It was as if Rommix was trying to brush something off its chest. Which it was!

No one had time to chat as the claw swung closer. Mason, Hanna and Kai ducked. But Zoe made the mistake of jumping. She flew into the air.

"Oh no, no, no!" Zoe muttered.

She had forgotten about her magnetic boots. And that she was standing on a vertical surface. Now, she was falling down the side of the robot. Straight towards the ground below!

CHAPTER 7

IN AGAIN

WHHHHIP!

Kai's ninja shot his grappler. It caught the foot of
Zoe's avatar in mid-air. Kai reeled her in like a fish.

> **ZKatt:** thx!! forgot we were on the side of a robot!

> **K-EYE:** I got your back! Or your foot!

> **ZKatt:** lol

"And that, Z-peeps, is why I have the best team
in OW," Zoe told her followers.

She swung back to the others. Her mag boots
locked her into place. But she wasn't out of danger yet.

The robot's claw swung forwards. Rommix was still trying to swat the players off its chest.

WHOOOOOOSH!

Zoe ducked this time. So did the others.

Then four drones flew in. And two laser turrets rose up. The squad was under attack from all sides!

ZKatt: maybe leaving the shortcut wuz a bad idea

hanna_banana: dont think so, look!!!

Hanna was moving towards another green hatch. She blew it open with a rocket. Behind it was a tunnel.

The squad made a run for it. Zoe shielded them as best she could from the attacks. Still, their health was dropping fast. But they made it down the hatch. Kai got busy passing out med packs.

hanna_banana: thx!!!

MACE1: check it!!!

Mason's avatar walked into the hall. He stopped by a huge weapon on the wall. It was a futuristic rifle with two large barrels.

K-EYE: Whoa. That's serious firepower.

hanna_banana: gotta b for somthng big!!!

ZKatt: that has u written all over it H

hanna_banana: naw i like my rockets

MACE1: u shud take it Z

ZKatt: me?

MACE1: oh yeah. levl up yur streaming!

Zoe grabbed the weapon. "Check out the new gear," she told her followers. "Only two shots, though. I don't know what it's for. But I bet we're about to find out!"

The squad went down the twisting hall. Then a thin robotic leg poked out from around a corner. More legs followed. A new enemy skittered out into the open. Then a second. Spider-bots!

ZZZT! ZZZT! Their red eyes blasted the squad with lasers.

Zoe raised her new weapon. Two shots. Two spiders. Was this really what the big shooter was for? But she held back, waiting.

Luckily, the spider-bots were no match for Hanna and Mason. They blasted the bots. Zoe put the shooter away. She would save it for later.

It wasn't long before the hall ended. It came to another hatch. The squad climbed out and ran to a nearby save point.

ZKatt: gr8! we r on the robots back! just like the shortcut with TTT. But higher up. so even better!

hanna_banana: SO CLOSE! lets take it down!!!

MACE1: srry, i gotta bail

hanna_banana: rly???

MACE1: Dev is being a pain

ZKatt: probs 4 the best. my dad stopped by and heard me talkin about getting n2 the robot head

hanna_banana: lol

ZKatt: should go xplain im not crazy

K-EYE: Doesn't help your case about going pro huh?

ZKatt: lol def not

MACE1: itll b fine. l8r

hanna_banana: ttfn!!!

K-EYE: We'll beat this thing tomorrow for sure.

Zoe left the mission. She opened her mouth to sign off to her followers. Then a DM box popped up on her screen. It was from TerryT3.

TerryT3: ZKatt! We're finishing the OW bot level. Wanna help again?

Zoe held her breath. Her hands froze over the keyboard. She didn't know what to do.

CHAPTER 8

BIG DECISION

Zoe stared at the DM from TerryT3. She knew she had promised not to play ahead. But she hadn't thought Triple-T would ask again. Beating the level with them would lead to a huge boost in followers. For sure!

She couldn't just say no. Her friends would get that, right? But her stomach twisted at the thought.

She needed a second opinion.

"Guess what, peeps?" Zoe asked her followers. "Triple-T just asked me to join them again. To finish this level. What do you think? Should I do it? Or should I finish with my friends?"

Zoe read their chats.

gandalf: ttt 4 me!

RedRhino44: TTT no contest

FlyAway: K-EYE saved u from fallng tho

pink22: shud b TTTZ!

wurmee: go w/ Ts!

DRRY: TTT!!!

BossFght: tuff call ZKatt

lemonHD: your squad is such a good team tho

Wnd-R-Boy: Triple-T!!!

Zoe scrolled through the replies. "Wow," she said. "Lots of votes for Triple-T."

She bit her lip. Something about that didn't sit right with her.

"Playing with a pro team *was* amazing. Really stretched my skills," Zoe added. She breathed deep. "But . . . I think I'm going to wait for my squad."

DRRY: TTT!!!

josh09: uhm... rlly?

lemonHD: good call Z!!

wurmee: WHUT???

SupMn10: wrong move

FlyAway: yay!

gandalf: why tho?

"I'll tell you why," Zoe said. She sat up straight. She felt better about her choice already. "Gaming for me is more than winning or levelling up. Or even going pro. It's about friendship." She smiled. "I know, super cheesy. And you get a pass on flaming me for that one. But I'm going to keep my promise. I am going to finish with my friends."

She leaned closer to her webcam. "If you can't wait to see Rommix go down? Then check out the Triple-T stream," she said. "Otherwise, join me and my squad tomorrow."

Zoe ended her stream. She let out another long breath. She started typing a reply to TerryT3. But she stopped as something caught her eye. Her dad stood in the doorway again.

"That was quite the speech," he said.

Zoe cringed. "I didn't know you were there."

Dad smiled. "I'm glad I was. Turning down those T guys? I guess your online friendships are important. A lot deeper than I thought."

Zoe nodded. "That's what I was trying to say."

Dad rubbed his neck. "I don't really understand all this streaming, gaming, chatting stuff," he said. "But I guess we can talk more about going pro." He held up a hand. "Just talk for now."

Zoe grinned. "Thanks, Dad."

He nodded and left the doorway.

Zoe couldn't stop smiling. She turned to finish her reply to TerryT3. He sent her another before she was through.

TerryT3: Great stream ZKatt! Big respect for stickin with yur crew. We'll hit you up again soon. We need more gamers like you.

CHAPTER 9

EYES ON THE PRIZE

The next night, Zoe met the squad at their last save point. They weren't under attack. So they had a chance to chat.

hanna_banana: and THEN TerryT3 said they need more gamers like Z!!!

MACE1: WHAAAATT

K-EYE: No way!

ZKatt: hey i wuz going 2 tell them!!

hanna_banana: sry!!! 2 good 2 keep in!!!

MACE1: srsly wow!

ZKatt: i know right??

hanna_banana: <3

K-EYE: You should've played with TTT.

MACE1: K!!

K-EYE: I mean I'm glad you didn't. But we would've understood.

MACE1: I gess so

hanna_banana: not me!!! lol!!! ok u GOTTA tell the other news Z

MACE1: ??

ZKatt: dad says we cn talk bout going pro

K-EYE: Congrats!

ZKatt: jst talk 4 now but still, pretty awesome!!

hanna_banana: knew u would wear him down ;)

MACE1: b4 u go pro, wanna finish ths level?

ZKatt: lol YES!

Zoe began her live stream. "Okay, Z-peeps! If you've stuck with me this far, my squad is not gonna let you down," she told them. "Here we go for the final attack!"

The squad started up the robot's back. After only a few steps, turrets rose from hidden hatches.

TZZZT! TZZZT!

The squad took cover. Mason and Hanna blasted the turrets.

But then drones flew overhead. More turrets rose up. Spider-bots crawled out.

WOMP! Zoe put up her shield. Her team sprang into action.

"We have to be close," Zoe told her followers. "Rommix is throwing everything it has at us!"

K-EYE: This is brutal! Time to use the big weapon?

ZKatt: dunno, only has 2 shots

MACE1: save it. H and i can handle things

hanna_banana: thats right!!!

MACE1: just shield and keep health, ammo comin

K-EYE: Will do!

TZZZT! TZZZT! BAM! FWOOOSH! FWOOOSH! TZZZT! BAM!

Mason and Hanna fired back at the threats. Zoe zipped around with her shield and blocked attacks. Kai rushed in with med packs and ammo.

Finally, the last enemy was destroyed. The squad kept walking up the robot's back. The head was closer than ever now.

MACE1: theres gotta b a hatch up here

hanna_banana: fyi only got 1 rocket left

K-EYE: No more in my supply either.

MACE1: thn save it 4 the hatch

ZKatt: dont see 1 yet tho. probs on top of its head?

They moved closer still. Just then, Rommix spun its head around. Its red eyes locked onto the squad. They glowed brightly.

K-EYE: UM

hanna_banana: thts not good!!!

MACE1: LOOK OUT

ZZZZZROP!

Giant lasers blasted from the robot's eyes.

CHAPTER 10

BIG FINISH

The squad ducked under Zoe's shield just as the lasers hit. The shield held. Barely. The powerful beams drained most of its energy.

The attack ended, and Mason stepped forward. He fired his laser rifle. **_ZZR! ZZR!_** Direct hits!

But the eyes showed no damage. They slowly began to glow again. Charging for another attack.

ZKatt: K pwr pack!

K-EYE: Last one!

MACE1: forget the shield and tke the shot Z!
use the new 2shooter!

Zoe had been focused on her shield's low power. She had completely blanked on the special weapon from earlier! She lowered the shield. Took out the shooter. She couldn't use both at the same time.

"Okay," she told her followers. "Two shots. Two eyes. It has to be time for this bad boy, right?"

Zoe fired.

WOAAAAAAP! A fat beam of electric plasma burst from the barrel.

KA-VOOM! The right eye exploded.

hanna_banana: WOOT!!!

MACE1: go 4 the othr 1

K-EYE: Look out!

The left eye fired! **ZZZZZROP!**

Zoe switched back to her shield. It blocked the beam. The shield's power dropped by a third.

Zoe was about to switch to the shooter. But the eye was already glowing again.

ZZZZZROP! Another blast hit Zoe's shield.

MACE1: get it!

ZKatt: cant fire and hold the shield

hanna_banana: the bot is shooting fastr now!!!

K-EYE: Maybe we can dodge it?

ZKatt: 2 risky, someone else has 2 take the shot while i shield

MACE1: H is best @ long range

hanna_banana: sure?

ZKatt: def! go 4 it!

Zoe passed the weapon to Hanna. The robot eye glowed. Hanna stepped out from the shield and fired.

WOAAAAAP! KA-VOOM!

Smoke filled Zoe's screen. The cloud slowly cleared. The last eye was gone!

MACE1: GG!!!!

K-EYE: YEAH!

ZKatt: knew u were the best 4 the job!

hanna_banana: can i have 1 of these evry mission??

The squad easily walked up the head. Sure enough, a green hatch was at the top. Hanna blasted it open with her last rocket. The players dropped inside.

They landed in a round room. Four seats lined the walls. In the centre was a tall table. It held a big red button.

hanna_banana: think we have 2 push the button. but im no pro gamer tho lol

ZKatt: lol me neither! yet!

K-EYE: So who gets the honour?

MACE1: Z. her stream aftr all

ZKatt: thx!

MACE1: everyone else buckle up!

The others strapped into the seats. Zoe stepped forwards. **THUNK!** She pressed the button. Then she ran to the last seat. The room shook around them.

> **K-EYE:** This is going to be a blast!
>
> **MACE1:** dude ugh
>
> **hanna_banana:** lol!!!

Zoe's screen filled with a cut scene. It showed Rommix from far away. Almost as far away as when they had started the level. But now, the giant robot loomed right next to the city. Then –

BOOF! BOOM! BAM! BOOM!

Small explosions erupted all over the robot's body. **FOOOOSH!** Then its head shot off. Jets of flame sent it rocketing higher and higher.

"Whoa! How cool is this?" Zoe asked her followers. "Bye-bye, Rommix! You're not destroying the city of Lexira today! Do I have the best squad or what?"

The jet flames died out. **FWOOMP!** A parachute burst from the robot head. The metal piece slowly floated to the ground.

The cut scene ended. The green hatch opened, and Zoe's squad climbed out.

KA-THOOOOM!

Then the robot's body blew into a million pieces behind them.

K-EYE: Another OW level down!

MACE1: AAAAW YEAH! GG!

hanna_banana: best OW squad evr!!!

K-EYE: Hope you'll still play with us after you go pro Z!

ZKatt: lol I prmse 2 ALWAYS play with u guys!!

Zoe grinned. That was a promise she knew she would never have trouble keeping!

BONUS ROUND

1. Describe how Zoe felt when her dad said she needed to have normal friendships. What in the text makes you think that? How would you have felt?

2. Zoe has big dreams of becoming a pro gamer. At first, her dad wasn't so sure about her goal. When you disagree with the adults in your life, how do you handle it?

3. Zoe told her squad that she had played ahead with the Triple-T gamers. How did her friends react to the news? How did she think they would react? Point to examples from the text to support your answer.

4. Think of a time when you felt hurt by a friend. Did you talk with your friend about it? How did it go? If you could go back, would you do anything differently?

5. Imagine if Zoe did play with Triple-T when they asked the second time. How do you think her squad would have reacted? Write out the chat.

6. What actions and qualities make a true friend? Write a list.

TAKING CARE

In real life, there may not be levels to beat. Or bosses to battle. But it can still be tough. Equip yourself with the tools and knowledge to take care of your mental health. Check out the online resources below. And don't ever be afraid to ask for help from friends, family or trusted adults.

BBC Bitesize:
www.bbc.co.uk/bitesize/articles/zmvt6g8

BBC Children in Need:
www.bbcchildreninneed.co.uk

Childline:
www.childline.org.uk

Health For Teens:
www.healthforteens.co.uk

Mental Health Foundation:
www.mentalhealth.org.uk

NHS Mental Health:
www.nhs.uk/mental-health/children-and-young-adults/mental-health-support/

Young Minds:
www.youngminds.org.uk/young-person/

GLOSSARY

avatar character in a video game, chat room, app or other computer program that stands for and is controlled by a person

explode blow apart with a loud bang and great force

focus keep all your attention on something

futuristic high-tech or very strange and modern looking, as if it comes from the future

grappler device that has a hook connected to the end of a rope, used for grabbing onto objects

hatch opening in a floor, deck, wall or ceiling; the door that covers this opening can also be called a hatch

lumbering moving slowly and heavily

mission planned job or task

overpass bridge that carries a road over another road

rubble pieces of a building or other structure that is being destroyed

sponsor company that pays to have special adverts shown by a person or during an event

turret structure that holds a weapon in one fixed spot, but that can be turned in any direction

THE AUTHOR

MICHAEL ANTHONY STEELE has been in the entertainment industry for more than 27 years, writing for television, films and video games. He has written more than 120 books for exciting characters and brands, including Batman, Superman, Wonder Woman, Spider-Man, Shrek and Scooby-Doo. Steele lives on a ranch in Texas, USA, but he enjoys meeting readers when he goes to visit schools and libraries across the United States. For more information, visit MichaelAnthonySteele.com.

THE ILLUSTRATOR

MIKE LAUGHEAD is a comics creator and illustrator of children's books, T-shirts, book covers and other fun things in the children's market. He has been doing that for almost 20 years. Mike is also an illustration instructor at Brigham Young University-Idaho, USA. He lives in Idaho with his amazing wife and three wonderful daughters. To see his portfolio, visit shannonassociates.com/mikelaughead

►► READ THEM ALL! ◄◄